P9-BZJ-046

Beach Party

Beach Party

Adapted by Jane Mason and Sara Hines Stephens

Based on "Backpack" written by Dan Schneider
"Little Beach Party" written by Steve Holland

Based on *Zoey 101* created by Dan Schneider

SCHOLASTIC INC.

New York   Toronto   London   Auckland   Sydney
Mexico City   New Delhi   Hong Kong   Buenos Aires

If you purchased this book without a cover, you should be aware that this book is stolen property. It was reported as "unsold and destroyed" to the publisher, and neither the author nor the publisher has received any payment for this "stripped book."

No part of this publication may be reproduced, stored in a retrieval system, or transmitted in any form or by any means, electronic, mechanical, photocopying, recording, or otherwise, without written permission of the publisher. For information regarding permission, write to Scholastic Inc., Attention: Permissions Department, 557 Broadway, New York, NY 10012.

ISBN 0-439-83160-1

© 2006 ApolloMedia. All Rights Reserved.
Nickelodeon, *Zoey 101*, and all related titles, logos, and characters are trademarks of Viacom International Inc.

Published by Scholastic Inc. All rights reserved.

SCHOLASTIC and associated logos are trademarks and/or registered trademarks of Scholastic Inc.

12 11 10 9 8 7 6 5 4 3 2 1   6 7 8 9 10 11/0

Printed in the U.S.A.

First printing, February 2006

Goo-Popped

The bookstore at Pacific Coast Academy was not your run-of-the-mill bookstore and mini-mart. no way. It was more like a mega-mini-mart. Beyond the usual staples and snacks, pencils and tacks, they had mags and backpacks, and everything in between.

It was the place to go if you were cold, or hungry, or just needed to catch up on the latest issue of *Teen Girl*. Which is exactly what Chase Matthews and Michael Barrett were doing.

"Okay, you're having a slumber party, and your best friend dares you to call the boy you have a crush on. What do you do?" Chase read the question from the teen column aloud to Michael.

The boys were quiet for a moment while they thought about their answers.

"That depends." Michael pointed at Chase,

considering his options carefully. There were some vari-ables. This was no simple-answer question. "How cute is the boy?" he asked, raising his eyebrows.

Before Chase could answer, they were interrupted by a girl's voice. "Okay, why are you guys reading *Teen Girl* magazine?" a cute girl asked from the next aisle over. It was Zoey Brooks, Chase and Michael's good friend, and she had heard everything. She was suddenly stand-ing in front of them, wearing a pink shirt with stripes down the sleeves. She was holding a case of water and looking at them like they were a little nuts.

"To learn stuff," Chase answered with a shrug. It was research — it seemed kind of obvious, didn't it?

"About what?" Zoey asked.

"Teen girls," Chase said. Zoey was usually really smart, but duh.

"Ooooh," Zoey said, getting it. She smirked at the guys. It's not like girls were that hard to figure out. But, whatever.

"All right," Michael said, returning to the business at hand. He still could not decide what to do about the slumber-party conundrum, but he was ready for more. "Skip to the next one," he prompted Chase.

"Okay, okay, ummmm . . ." Chase scanned the page,

looking for another question. "Ooh!" He practically squealed when he spotted a good one. "Here we go. Your best friend borrows your lip gloss *without asking,*" he finished.

Michael clutched his heart and gasped, imagining the horror of the situation. Zoey rolled her eyes and shook her head.

"Yeah, yeah." Chase nodded with understanding before going on. "Okay, so do you: A: get a new best friend, B: push her down a flight of stairs, or C —"

"What?!" Zoey interrupted. "It doesn't say that!" She had read enough girl mags to know that they didn't condone violence.

"I know, but I feel it should definitely be an option," Chase explained. "After all, the girl did use your gloss *without* asking."

"Well, I say B," Michael said, gesturing to himself to show the significance of his thoughts on the matter. "Down the stairs she goes." He pantomimed a good shove, and the boys busted up.

Zoey had to laugh, too. "You guys are sick," she said, tossing her blond hair.

"Yeah," Chase agreed.

"We pretty much are," Michael admitted, nodding

and scoping out the magazine shelf for something else to read.

"Hey, Zo'?" Nicole Bristow, one of Zoey's best friends and also her roommate, was at the counter with a pile of healthy snacks. She and Zoey were picking up dorm provisions. Finals were wiping out their rations — nothing like cramming for tests and cramming your face at the same time. "They don't have any grapes," Nicole shouted over the shelves to Zoey. She knew Zoey was crazy for grapes. She said they made good snacks and good ammunition. "Do you want some raisins?" she asked.

Zoey made a face. "No, I hate raisins," she answered, looking horrified at the suggestion.

"Why do you hate raisins?" Michael asked, looking baffled. Who hated raisins? What was there to hate? Weren't they just dried grapes?

Scrunching up her nose, Zoey shook her head with distaste. "They're all wrinkly. I feel like I'm eating little-bitty old people."

Both the boys looked up from their reading. Michael looked at Chase. Chase looked at Michael.

"And *we're* sick?" Chase asked.

At the counter, a big glass jar caught Nicole's eye. "Ohh!" she squealed to Marty, the store manager. "You have little Goo Pops!" She thought she knew everything that the store carried — she considered herself the PCA bookstore's shopping expert.

"Yeah, we just got 'em in." Marty paused in his restocking to smile at Nicole and cock an eyebrow. "You want some Goo?" he asked.

"Yeah, I wanna buy raspberry and lime." Nicole leaned forward to pick her two favorite flavors out of the jar. Luckily, they were also her favorite colors and looked color-coordinated *and* were delicious together. One even matched her T-shirt! She admired the little tubes of colorful gel before calling Zoey over to show her. "Hey, Zoey, come over here! You've gotta taste this."

Zoey carried her case of water over to the counter and set it down. "What is it?" she asked. Nicole handed her a tube, and she turned it over in her hand.

"Goo Pops. They're awesome," Nicole told her excitedly.

"How do I open it?" Zoey turned the plastic tube over in her hand. There didn't seem to be a top or a bottom or an opening of any kind.

"Oh, easy," Nicole took the tube out of her hand. "You just bite the tip." Nicole nibbled delicately on the plastic wrapper of her Goo Pop. "Then you just squeeze." It was simple. But when Nicole squeezed, nothing came out. "Wait, it's not coming out." She bit again, more roughly, and squeezed harder. And harder. Suddenly, a giant sticky squirt of red gel shot out of the plastic tube, across the counter, and all over a backpack hanging on the wall. The poor pack looked like it had been wounded. Nicole gasped and covered her mouth, horrified.

"It came out," Zoey deadpanned.

Nicole looked at Zoey, her face showing pure panic. Then she looked up at Marty, who was eyeing her over the tops of his glasses. He did *not* look pleased. Glancing over at the gooped-up backpack, Nicole silently prayed that raspberry Goo didn't stain.

Her prayer went unanswered. Several minutes of intense scrubbing later, Marty was still trying to get the Goo off the backpack. He'd found a rag and some cleaner, but the sticky stuff that had finally come out of the tube did not want to come out of the backpack. The Goo had gone, but the red stain remained.

Marty stopped his fruitless cleaning and looked at the kids gathered at the register — Zoey, Michael, Chase, and Nicole.

Nicole bit her lip nervously. This was definitely not looking good for her. "Well?" she asked, not really wanting to know what would happen next.

Marty sighed. "I'm sorry," he said, shaking his

head. His tone was apologetic. The news was not good. "It won't come out. I'm afraid you're gonna have to buy the backpack."

"Aw, man," Nicole fretted. A backpack was the last thing she wanted to buy. She had several bags already, and this backpack was damaged!

"How much is it?" Zoey asked, getting right to the nitty-gritty.

Marty checked the tag. "With tax, it's fifty dollars," he reported.

"Owww!" Nicole said, feeling the hit to her wallet. Fifty dollars was a lot of money. This stank. "I don't have fifty bucks." The snacks alone had wiped out all the money she had left for the month.

"Well, maybe you can borrow it from a friend," Marty suggested.

Nicole turned her big, pleading brown eyes on Michael and Chase, who were standing right behind her.

Chase looked around the bookstore like he had forgotten Nicole was in front of him. Then he checked his watch. "Whoa!" he exclaimed. "Look at the time!"

Michael leaned over to look at Chase's watch. "We're late!" he exclaimed. For what, he had no idea. But it didn't matter. They had to get out of there!

Michael turned to leave, but was headed in the wrong direction! Chase tugged on his sleeve, and they raced out of the school store without looking back.

Nicole sighed. No luck there. She put her purse on the counter and began to dig through it. Somewhere in here she had some emergency cash. Her mom told her not to spend it unless there was a serious emergency. Unfortunately, this was turning into one. Who knew what Marty would do if she couldn't pay for the backpack? He might make her work in the store until she graduated!

"I have thirty," Nicole said, holding up the bills she'd found. It wasn't enough, but it was something.

With a sigh, Zoey opened her own wallet. She pulled out a twenty. Her last. "I have twenty," she said a little sadly.

"Not anymore." Nicole snatched the bill out of her friend's hand and handed all of their cash over to Marty. Then she turned back to Zoey. "Thanks, Zoey. I really feel bad."

"Here." Zoey was sad to part with her cash, but the Goo stain had been an accident, and she didn't want her friend to feel too awful. "Have another Goo Pop." She offered Nicole the candy.

"Thanks." Nicole took it from her cautiously. "I don't know why that other one squirted out like that."

8

Nicole bit the top of the pop. "All I did was squeeze a little like this —" Nicole squeezed once more to demonstrate.

Goo shot out of the container and onto Zoey's face, in a gloppy gel streak that started at Zoey's forehead and dripped off her chin.

Great, Zoey thought. *Green looks terrible on me.*

CHAPTER 2

B'napple Bonkers

Quinn Pensky, Pacific Coast Academy's own resident science genius, walked around a large, tropical-looking tree, examining it and beaming. In her hand she carried a small tape recorder, which she spoke into as necessary. "Leaf quality," she reported, "firm, yet spongy." She stroked the broad leaves tenderly and grinned. So far, her experiment was going perfectly! The six-foot tree was laden with strange-looking banana-shaped fruit and grew right outside a dorm on the PCA campus.

"Hey, Quinn," Michael said, approaching cautiously. It was always best to use a little caution when dealing with Quinn. You never knew if she wanted to recruit you as a subject for one of her Quinnventions.

"What's up?" Chase asked.

"This!" Quinn pointed proudly to the fruit tree and

waited for the guys to applaud or turn cartwheels or something. No reaction. Couldn't they see they were standing in front of a scientific success story?

The boys exchanged glances. Judging from the look of pride on her face, Quinn was thinking this was a much bigger deal than some ordinary fruit tree. But Michael didn't get it. "A banana tree?" he asked. That was nothing new.

"It was." Quinn nodded, the corners of her mouth turning up into a proud smile. "Until I altered its genetic structure."

"So . . . it's not a banana tree anymore?" Chase asked skeptically, casually looking for cover in case he needed to run for it. This was already sounding pretty weird. And knowing Quinn . . .

"No, sir," Quinn said proudly. "Now it's a b'napple tree."

"Sure." Chase smiled and nodded. It was best to remain calm and humor folks who had gone around the bend. He looked at Michael, trying to signal him that they should back away. Slowly.

"You see," Quinn explained, "my two favorite fruits of all time are the banana" — she rifled through her bag and held up a visual aid, in case the guys didn't know what a banana looked like — "and the apple." Again with the visual aid. "So, I crossbred their DNA to create the first b'napple tree." Quinn gave the green fruit hanging in bunches on the tree a tender pat. "When these babies turn red they'll be ready for eating."

"So, lemme get this straight," Michael said. "You're growin' a new fruit that's half apple and half banana?"

"That is correct," Quinn said, still holding her ordinary apple and banana and nodding like a college professor who had just answered an important scientific question.

Michael could not hold it in. He laughed out loud. Even Chase let out a chuckle.

Quinn couldn't believe these bozos. What were they laughing at? Didn't they know an important scientific discovery when they saw one? "Fine," she said huffily. "Laugh now. But when these babies ripen and turn red, get ready for the best fruit experience of your lifetime." She closed her eyes and let her imagination go. She could almost taste it already. It was going to be great!

"Okaaaay." Chase smiled and nodded. The time to get away was now. And quickly.

"We'll be ready," Michael assured Quinn. "Later."

"See ya." Chase waved, checking over his shoulder as he and Michael made a safe getaway. Behind them, Quinn took a bite of her apple and a bite of her banana and chewed them together to get a personal b'napple preview.

"Mmmm." It was going to be better than any fruit experience she'd ever had. It was going to be truly awesome! Taking a deep breath, she turned to her tree. "Hurry up and mature." Quinn spoke softly to the young fruit. "I can't wait!" Before walking away from the unripe b'napples to enjoy her two fruits, she quickly leaned in and kissed them good-bye.

The girls' lounge was bustling with students. Some were studying. Some were lounging. Some were trying to find a good station to listen to on a hopelessly retro stereo that only seemed to get static. And one girl, Nicole, was glaring at a hopelessly stained backpack.

"Stupid backpack." Nicole stared at the waste of fifty bucks. "Stupid Goo Pop stain." She rubbed at the embedded stain.

"Y'know, you could still use the backpack," Zoey said, looking up from her laptop. She was sitting next to her roomie on one of the couches.

"No, I can't." Even if Nicole had wanted the backpack, there was no way she was going to walk around with it all Goo'd upon. "It's all . . ." She couldn't even find a word to describe the offensiveness of the bag.

"Stupid?" Zoey finished the sentence for her.

"Yeah." Nicole sighed. And it was making her cranky. Really cranky. Or maybe it was all the static that was getting on her nerves. "Would you guys just pick a station already?" Nicole snapped at Dana Cruz, Zoey and Nicole's other roommate, who was sitting with another girl turning the dial on the ancient stereo in search of a station. "That static is driving me insane."

"I'm trying." Dana sounded exasperated as she fiddled with the knobs. She shared a room with Nicole, but not much else. The two were as different as night and day, and Dana was thinking she'd like to see Nicole do any better.

Just then, Chase and Michael walked in. "Chase, can you fix our stereo?" Dana asked, trying to sound a little sweet. It was not her style to be sweet or ask a guy to assist her, but stereos were not her area of expertise. And even a toddler knew that you usually got further if you asked nicely.

Chase was always game to help. He ambled over and tried his hand. "Man, how old is this thing?" he asked, eyeing the stereo. "It's like prehistoric."

"Yeah," Michael agreed. "It looks like it's from the eighties."

"Thanks," Dana said sarcastically as she watched

them fiddle in exactly the same way she and her friend had done. The only difference with their technique was that the guys gave up even faster than the girls had, and then walked over to join Zoey and Nicole.

"What's up, Zo'? Nicole?" Chase flopped down in a chair while Michael collapsed into the seat next to him.

"Nothin'." Zoey shrugged. "What're you guys up to?"

"About to catch a movie on campus," Chase said. He was hoping Zoey would want to come and was about to ask when Michael beat him to it.

"Yeah. We're seein' *Spider-Bat.* You wanna come with?" Michael looked excited about the new action-adventure.

"We can't," Nicole said loudly through bared teeth. It wasn't easy to make yourself heard over the racket still coming out of the stereo. Besides, she was feeling just plain angry.

"Okaay," Chase said, holding up his hands. Nicole was usually the cheerful one. "And why the screaming?"

"She's mad because we don't have any money left," Zoey explained.

"'Cause we had to spend it all on this stupid back-pack!" Nicole fumed. Standing up, she grabbed the pack by the straps, threw it into the wastepaper basket, stomped on it for good measure, and stormed upstairs. All of this hostility was bound to make her hair frizz and if there was one thing Nicole hated, it was frizzy hair.

Once again, Chase and Michael tiptoed away from a potentially volatile situation. On their way past the trash, they paused and looked at the can.

"Did you hear that, backpack?" Michael asked softly.

"Apparently," Chase addressed the book bag, "you're very stupid."

"Very," Michael reiterated before heading out.

"Later," Chase said to Zoey.

"Byeeeee." Zoey waved to her friends before getting up to retrieve the stupid pack. As she eyed it sitting on top of the wastebasket, a smile crept across her face. She had an idea. A good one.

Reclining in her top bunk, Nicole was listening to tunes on her tiny boom box, munching popcorn, and doing a little target practice. Every time she came across an unpopped kernel in her bowl, she put it in her homemade slingshot and sent it flying across the room to explode one of the balloons she had taped to the wall. She rarely missed. When she hit a balloon, it made a satisfying *bang*. And it kept her from breaking a tooth on a kernel. Talk about two birds with one stone.

"Hey," Zoey greeted her friend when she came into their room.

"Hey," Nicole said. She knew she did not sound like her usual bubbly self. She did not feel like her usual bubbly self, either. There was not a single bubbly part in her whole body. After a second, she found another kernel and let it fly. A balloon on the wall expired with a loud *bang*.

"Um, what are you doing?" Zoey asked.

"Shooting unpopped popcorn kernels at balloons," Nicole explained.

"That's how you're spending your Friday night?" Zoey could hardly believe it. Nicole was a social butterfly. Something was up with this girl. That backpack had really gotten her down. Zoey grabbed a handful of popcorn and munched while she considered the situation.

"It's all I can afford to do," Nicole said, pouting. "Where have you been all night?"

"Making something." Zoey could not wait a moment longer for her big reveal. This just *had* to cheer up Nicole. She walked over to the door, reached outside, and pulled in her creation . . . well, *re*-creation. "Ta-daaa!"

17

Zoey held up the world's coolest backpack for her friend to see.

In a second, the old bubbly, bouncy, happy Nicole was back. "Whoa! That is such a cool backpack!" she squealed, abandoning her popcorn and slingshot and hopping off the high bunk to get a closer look.

"I'm glad you think so." Zoey beamed. "'Cause it's yours."

"Huh?" Nicole was confused. She had never seen the pack before. It was greenish, like the one at the bookstore, but this one was covered in all kinds of patches, and pins of hearts and flowers, and other cool designs, like some sort of fabric collage. It was practically art.

"It's the one you bought this afternoon," Zoey explained.

Nicole grabbed the pack and looked closer. At first she could not believe it, but upon inspection, she realized it was true. "It is! How'd you do this?" she asked, astounded.

"I just did it." Zoey shrugged modestly.

"Wow, you covered up the Goo and everything." Nicole searched carefully but could not see the stain under the awesome art.

Zoey was glad Nicole noticed. "Yep! No more Goo."

"Ooh." Nicole was speechless as she hugged the backpack.

The door to their dorm room opened again and Quinn marched in with a big pink banana in her hand. "It's pink," she cried excitedly, holding the fruit out for the girls to see. "My b'napple is pink!"

Zoey and Nicole stared at Quinn and the pink fruit, puzzled. Zoey could tell she was totally psyched, but she had no idea what the girl was talking about. "What does that mean?" Zoey asked.

"Soon they'll be ripe and red, and I will have successfully crossbred the banana and the apple to create the best fruit in the universe!" She was so excited, her many long thin braids looked like they were dancing on her head, and she sounded like she might explode.

Zoey watched, stunned, as Quinn finished her proclamation and spun out of the room. A second later, Quinn was back. "Cool backpack," she said, sticking her head through the door for a split second. She was gone again before Zoey could even say thanks.

CHAPTER 3

What's the Big Idea?

When the bell rang, students emptied out of the math building like they were doing a fire drill. Chase followed the throng of students out into the ocean air. As far as he was concerned, it was never too soon to evacuate his geometry class.

"Okay, geometry is impossible," he vented his frustrations to Zoey, Dana, Nicole, and anybody else who would listen, as they headed up a narrow path. "I mean, what is a trapezoid?" It sounded like a jail for aliens.

"It's a quadrilateral with two parallel sides," Zoey said quickly, turning back to her friend. Where had Chase been for the last hour?

"But I —" Even though Zoey had answered his question, Chase looked more confused than ever. "I thought that was a rhombus."

"Nooo." Dana rolled her eyes as she followed behind her friends. "Weren't you listening in class?"

"A rhombus is an equilateral parallelogram," Nicole explained. That was an easy one. She had her new backpack slung over her shoulder and any sign of crankiness from the previous day had burned off with the morning fog.

"Okay." Chase took a deep breath. Everyone was getting this but him. "But what is a parallelogram?"

"I'm not telling you again." Zoey sighed. She had completely given up. Chase needed more help than she could offer when it came to math. "Look in your textbook." Maybe if he looked it up himself the information would stick.

While Chase rifled through pages, Vicki stopped Nicole on the path. "Hey, Nicole, where'd you get that backpack?" she asked. Her eyes were wide as she stared at the truly original creation on Nicole's back.

"Oh, Zoey made it." Nicole modeled the pack for her admirer.

"Really?" Vicki looked like she could hardly believe it.

"Yeah." Zoey nodded and gave a small smile. Even she had to admit the pack had turned out very cool.

"I want one!" Vicki said, looking at the pack excitedly.

"Y'know, these are pretty cool." Chase took a closer look at Nicole's new pack. "You should make a guy's one."

"Totally," Vicki agreed.

Inside Zoey's head, the gears were turning. It wasn't a bad idea. "Okay." Zoey reached for Chase's pack. "Gimme."

Chase shrugged and handed his PCA bag over, still full.

"Don't you wanna get your books out so you can study later?" Zoey asked. Finals were not far off and Chase was not exactly working on extra credit.

"Uh, gross," Chase declined. If he had a chance to get a break from his homework he'd take it, no questions asked.

"Okay." Zoey laughed. No wonder he couldn't tell a rhombus from a trapezoid! "I'll call you when it's ready."

"Cool." As Zoey and the girls walked off with his backpack in hand, Chase felt lighter than he had in days — like he had all the time in the world to go over his geometry. Except . . . "Oh, wait!" he shouted. "What's a parallelogram?!"

"It's a four-sided plane figure with opposite parallel

sides. Doy!" Some puny sixth grader with glasses walked by and schooled Chase, pausing briefly before moving on. "Oh, yeah?" Chase shouted after him racking his brain for a snappy retort. "Well, I'm taller than you!"

Small tubes of paint, glue, and glitter lined the round green table where Zoey worked. Nicole, Chase, and a few girls in the lounge watched while she put the crowning touches on Chase's bag. She pinned on a medal beside the appliqué of a rattlesnake. *Voilà!* The pack looked as cool as Nicole's, but this one was definitely for guys.

"Ohhhh-kay," Zoey said, finishing up. "Whaddya think?" She held the bag up and waited for a response. They had to love it. She loved it. It looked terrific!

"Awesome." Chase took the bag and turned it over in his hands. It was completely transformed. "Are you sure this is the same backpack?" he asked.

"Of course!" Zoey looked at Chase like he was crazy. Did he think she had money to buy a new one?

"Oh, yeah, there's the bullet hole." Chase pointed to an invisible hole near the top. Then he glanced up at all of the wide eyes around him. "Kidding," he assured them.

Vicki and her friend Annie looked on enviously as

Chase shouldered his bag. They could not get over Zoey's handiwork. "Zoey, these are so cool. When are you gonna do mine?" Vicki asked.

"And mine!" Annie put in.

The orders were coming fast and furious! "Soon, I promise," Zoey said. But she wasn't sure how soon she could get to them, with homework, basketball, and finals looming and all.

Suddenly, Nicole's face lit up. "You know what, Zo'? You should sell these!"

"Hey, that's a great idea," Chase agreed. So did the rest of the crowd around the table.

"I know," Nicole said.

"Eh, I don't know." Zoey was just having a good time making stuff for her friends. She wasn't sure *other* people would want her packs.

"Seriously," Nicole said, "if these were in a store, people would totally buy 'em."

"Yeah, in a heartbeat," Vicki added.

"You really think so?" Zoey asked. Who would have thought a project she'd taken on to cover up a Goo stain would grow into — who knew what? She was so distracted by the thought of what it might lead to, she didn't notice Stacy, a senior, listening in on the whole conversation while she hung some flyers on the bulletin board. Neither did Chase.

"I'd buy one. Except, you know, I already got this one for free, so it'd be pretty silly for me to buy another one when I already, um —" The more Chase talked, the less sure he felt. Did he owe Zoey for this? "This is free, right?" he asked.

"I'll think about it," Zoey teased, lowering her eyebrows. Of course it was free. Chase was one of her best friends!

Everyone laughed as Stacy made her way up to the table. "Excuse me," she said, still holding her flyers. "Hi. Sorry to eavesdrop — I was just putting up these flyers for the senior bake sale. Um, Zoey, right?"

Zoey was a little surprised that the older girl knew her name. "Uh-huh." She nodded.

"Did you really make these backpacks?" Stacy asked, flipping her straight brown hair over her shoulder and admiring Chase's bag.

"Yeah." Zoey was humble, but they had turned out pretty great.

Nicole wasn't humble at all. She puffed out her chest like a proud mother hen. "How talented is she?" she crowed.

"Extremely." Stacy nodded in agreement. Then she pulled out a small digital camera. "Hey, do you mind if I take a couple of pics for the school paper?" she asked.

Zoey was flattered. It wasn't every day a senior girl wanted to do a write-up on you for the school newspaper. "Go ahead," she said, giving Stacy a little room to work.

"Great." Stacy snapped away. "This is so cool, really," she said again. "Great job."

"Hey, uh, do you wanna take a pic with the backpack on me?" Chase offered, getting into it. He held up his pack like a game-show model might.

Stacy looked at him like he was something she had just scraped off the bottom of her shoe. "Yeah, not really," she said, kind of harshly.

"Yeah, I—" Chase needed to save a little face here. But it wasn't going to happen. "I didn't want to," he said, feebly stepping away from his pack.

Stacy started taking pictures of the pack from all angles. "This is so genius. Let me see that one." She pointed at Nicole's and snapped off a few more shots. "Nice."

Pack Attack

Armed with her magnifying glass and mini tape recorder, Quinn approached her tree, ready to observe and report. The b'napple babies were ripening to an orangey red — not yet ripe, but not too far to go.

"It's been three weeks since my b'napple tree first fruited," she said into the tiny tape recorder. Then, poking a fruit, she continued her report. "Color: reddish-orange. Texture: smooth. Smell —" Quinn paused, leaned in, and took a big sniff — "b'napply," she announced with a giant grin.

She was almost through with her report when she noticed something on the ground. Something that should not have been there. "Wait. What's this?" Quinn bent over and picked up a mangled, half-ripe b'napple peel. She stared at it through her dark-rimmed glasses. Her smile faded. The look of horror that replaced it said more than words ever could. Who would do such a thing to her treasured fruit?

"Birds!" Quinn said aloud, suddenly realizing who was responsible. Seething, she turned her face to the sky — the horrible hunting ground of the enemy. "This isn't over! Nobody messes with my b'napples! Ya hear me?" she cried, shaking her fist at the sky. Then, turning back to her precious tree, Quinn spoke softly. "Don't worry, my little mutant fruits," she assured them. "I'll protect you."

"So what do you want to do tonight?" Across campus, Nicole and Zoey were strolling the grounds, trying to make a plan.

"I dunno." Zoey shrugged. "Rent a movie?"

"With what money?" Nicole asked.

Good point. "Oh, yeah." Zoey had almost forgotten how broke they both were. "Well, we could, um, shoot balloons with a slingshot?"

"I already shot 'em all. And balloons cost three bucks a bag. Man, it stinks bein' poor, doesn't it?" Nicole looked truly bummed out.

"Kinda," Zoey agreed, even though she knew they had no clue what it was really like to be poor. She was about to point out that at least they had clothes and food and a place to sleep, when something caught her eye. Two girls walked by with backpacks that looked a lot like Nicole's.

"Hey, did you see those backpacks?" Nicole asked.

"Yeah," Zoey said, puzzled. She hadn't made any more packs. Where did these others come from?

"I love it. Doncha just love it?" A girl named Kyle, who Zoey recognized from gym, walked by with another cool pack, showing it to a friend. Then *another* cool pack walked past on someone else's back.

Zoey looked at Nicole. Nicole looked as freaked as she felt. Something was definitely up.

"Okay, what is going on?" Nicole asked.

Zoey shook her head. She wished she knew. Taking a good look around, she spotted something across the courtyard — something that made her blood boil. It explained a lot. "That is." Zoey could not hide the annoyance in her voice as she pointed toward a table set up on the lawn complete with a rack, banner, and sign. "Come on."

Zoey marched toward the booth with Nicole right behind her. Stacy was seated at the decorated table. The rack behind her held dozens of Zoey-esque decorated packs being admired by a small crowd of kids. And a line of people stood in front of the table holding packs and waiting to fork over money to buy them. The sign on the table in front of the smug-looking senior read BACKPACKS BY STACY. What the sign forgot to mention was that the idea for the packs was Zoey's. And Zoey was steamed.

She stood there fuming, watching while Stacy took in cash hand over fist. Girls and guys alike were going ga-ga over *Zoey's* idea.

Finally, Stacy spotted them. She smiled like everything in the world was just peachy . "Oh, hi, girls! Hey, if you wanna buy one of my backpacks you better hurry! They're sellin' fast." She jerked her thumb over her shoulder toward the rack of packs and smiled like she was the star in a breath mint commercial.

Zoey's mouth fell open. She could not believe what she was seeing. Stacy was not even embarrassed or apologetic! Beside Zoey, Nicole stood with her mouth agape, too. They were mad. They were furious! And they were definitely *not* in any mood to buy backpacks.

Giving Stacy the eye, Zoey watched the customers clear out with hip backpacks slung on their shoulders. Stacy held a fistful of cash and had a smirk on her face. Zoey wanted to clobber the girl. She wanted to make the whole scene in front of her — including the awful girl — just disappear. Who would do such a thing?

Just then, Chase and Michael raced up behind her. "Hey, Zoey," Michael said breathlessly. He'd been running to keep up with Chase. The dude was a lot faster than he looked.

"What's goin' on?" Chase asked, looking around. It was another beautiful day at PCA and seeing Zoey made everything look a little bit brighter. Except that she looked, well, pretty much furious. Her usually ready smile was replaced with a really angry look — one he had not seen since Prank Week, when the boys TP'd the girls' dorm, and did not particularly want to see again. Suddenly, Chase was filled with panic. Was she mad at him? "What?!" he asked, already feeling a little defensive.

"That!" Nicole huffed, pointing to Stacy and her backpack booth. The stealing senior was still busy making cash, totally ignoring Zoey. Nicole glared. Unbelievable.

"Hey, I thought you said you didn't want to sell your backpacks," Chase said. Girls could really be fickle.

"I did. I mean I didn't. I mean, I did say that I didn't want to sell 'em!" She was so frustrated, she didn't make any sense!

"Wait," Michael said, getting the picture. "So, those aren't *your* backpacks?"

"No!" Zoey felt like she was going to explode.

All at once Chase understood why Zoey was mad, and he didn't blame her. What he was looking at was not cool. Not cool at all.

"That mean chick stole Zoey's idea!" Nicole blurted, just to make sure everyone was clear about what was going on.

Several yards away, Stacy cheerfully accepted more money from a happy customer. As the girl turned to leave, Stacy called out, "Oh, hey! There'll be more 'Backpacks by Stacy' in next week! Tell your friends!" She sounded like a used-car salesman.

That was it! Who did this girl think she was? Zoey walked up to the backpack booth and stood right in front of Stacy. She could not pretend like this was not happening and she wasn't going to let Stacy pretend it was okay. Nicole was by Zoey's side, and Chase and Michael were right behind her. "Ummm, hi?" she said a little sarcastically.

"Hi!" Stacy said, cheerfully plastering on a fake smile. What a phony. "Is there a problem?" The expression on her face was pure innocence.

"Yeah, there's a problem!" Nicole said, exasperated. Did this girl have amnesia? "You stole Zoey's backpack idea!"

Stacy blinked in surprise. "I'm sorry, I have no idea what you're talking about."

"Yeah, you do!" Zoey said. How could she not? She had taken a zillion photos of Zoey's backpacks. They were all there and they all saw it.

Stacy looked totally blank. Then she smiled and gestured to the packs behind her. "Would you like to buy one of my backpacks?" she asked.

Chase had had enough. What was with this girl? "Dude, we know these were Zoey's idea," he said flatly.

Stacy looked flustered — for about a second. Then suddenly, she said with a half smile, "I'm sorry, we're closed. Come back another day."

"You're not closed!" Nicole insisted. She had just finished selling a bunch of backpacks and had offered them one, too!

"Yeah, you're just a table." Michael gestured to the backpack setup. "You can't close a table."

Reaching down to the sign sitting on the table, Stacy turned it so that the word CLOSED faced Zoey and her friends. She ran her fingers across the front of the sign and smiled smugly.

"She closed the table," Michael said in disbelief. What was this girl's problem?

Zoey stared at the CLOSED sign. She looked up at Stacy's smirk. There was nothing more they could do — at least not now. "Let's get outta here," she said to her friends.

"Thank you!" Stacy called after them cattily. "Come again!"

Just keep walking, Zoey told herself. But she couldn't resist turning around one more time to glare at the senior who thought she could steal ideas and walk all over younger classmen. This was *not* over. Not by a long shot.

Sparking Ideas

Zoey sat at an outside lunch table feeling totally bummed out. Nicole and Dana sat on either side of her, quietly eating their food. Zoey wasn't hungry. Even her grapes did not look enticing. Everywhere she looked she saw Stacy's backpacks. They were the hottest thing on campus.

"Maybe you can sue her," Nicole suddenly blurted.

"I'm not gonna sue the girl," Zoey said.

"Why not?" Dana asked. After all, Stacy had clearly stolen Zoey's idea. And thieves should have to pay. Right?

"Because I'm thirteen, and thirteen-year-olds don't sue people," Zoey pointed out. She was as mad as her friends, but the solution didn't involve going to court.

"Well, they should," Nicole insisted. She looked across the table at Michael. "Michael, don't you think Zoey should sue that girl? Michael?"

Michael was so busy grooving to some music blasting through his headphones that he didn't hear a word Nicole was saying. He didn't see her, either. With his eyes closed, he jiggled his plate in time with the music.

Nicole was annoyed. Didn't Michael know they were in the middle of a crisis? Frustrated, she pulled her straw out of her drink and loaded it with a raisin. Then she gave a good blow and —

Thwap! It hit Michael right in the neck.

"Owwwww!" Michael complained, coming out of his groove session.

Zoey looked at Nicole, impressed. "Man, you're good with projectiles, aren't you?"

Nicole nodded, looking quite pleased with herself. She *was* really good with projectiles.

Michael, however, was not so pleased. He pulled the headphones out of his ears and glared at Nicole. "Did you just hit me with this raisin?" he asked incredulously. "You coulda put my eye out!"

"I was trying to get your attention," Nicole said in response.

"Well, excuse me, but I got thirty thousand songs to listen to in this thing." He pointed to his digital music player.

Dana raised an eyebrow. "Is that a new player?" she asked, sounding impressed. "How do you like it?"

"I love it, except for these headphones," he said, holding up the small white earpiece. "I hate stickin' these things in my ear, 'cause after a while it starts to hurt, ya know?"

Nicole let out a long puff of air. This conversation was getting way off track. "Can we talk about Zoey's backpack situation?" she said indignantly as Chase approached the table. Where were these people's heads? They had important things to discuss!

"You guys wanna talk backpacks?" Chase asked with a grimace. He held up the PCA newspaper. "Seen the school paper today?"

"Why?" Nicole asked. She didn't like the sound of that.

"What's in it?" Zoey asked. Even as she asked the question she had a sinking feeling that she didn't want to know the answer.

Chase let the paper fall to the table. "Oh, just a little article about Stacy's backpacks," he said sarcastically as he pulled out a chair and sat down.

"What?" Zoey asked. Things were going from bad to worse!

"Check the headline," Chase prompted, tossing the paper across the table. He hated being the bearer of bad news, and the sooner he got it over with, the better. Besides, Zoey deserved to know the truth.

Zoey picked up the paper and her jaw dropped. "Backpack Attack?!" she read aloud.

"Hey, that's really clever!" Nicole chirped, forgetting their situation for a second. Zoey's look brought her back to reality. The attack was on Zoey — or, at least, her idea! "Well, it rhymes," Nicole finished sheepishly.

"Oh, and it gets worse," Chase said, wanting to get all the bad news off his chest. "Stacy's backpacks? The PCA bookstore wants to start selling 'em." He held his breath, waiting for Zoey's response.

"No way," Michael said.

"Yeah way." Chase confirmed. "And they're gonna give her a big cut of the profits."

"No way!" Dana said again, only louder. This was out of control.

"Once again," Chase said. Were his friends suddenly hard of hearing? *"Yeah way."*

"Man, this is unbelievable," Michael said as he skimmed the newspaper article. "Stacy's gonna be rich."

"That headline should say, Stacy: Big Ol' Backpack

Stealer," Nicole said, pouting. She was still trying to make up for admiring the headline in the first place.

Everyone stared at her. Was that the best she could come up with?

"Or something clever," Nicole said more softly.

Chase settled into his chair and pulled off his Zoey backpack. "Well, at least *we* know these were Zoey's idea." He rubbed his neck and shoulders. "Ah man, books sure are heavy. Michael" — he looked pleadingly at his friend sitting next to him — "rub my shoulders."

Michael raised his dark eyebrows and tossed a french fry back onto his plate. "Have you lost your mind?" he asked. He was *not* Chase's masseur.

"C'mon, I hurt!" Chase cried. "Friends don't let other friends hurt."

Michael shot Chase a "give me a break" look. "Well, these headphones are hurtin' my ears." He lifted up an earbud for clarity. "What, you wanna massage my ear hole?!" he said mockingly, cocking his ear toward Chase. "Come on, massage it. Stick your finger in there."

Chase held up his hands in mock defense. "Ah!" he half shrieked. "I'll massage my own shoulders." He crossed his arms around his shoulders and began to rub.

Nicole rolled her eyes. Boys could be so goofy.

And they were in the middle of a crisis! "Zoey, are you just gonna let that nasty Stacy get rich off your idea?" She was surprised that Zoey wasn't putting up more of a fight. Zoey was not the kind of girl who sat around letting others take action.

But Zoey wasn't really listening. She was watching Chase rub his shoulders. She was watching Michael wince when he put his headphones in his ears. She was thinking and she was having ideas. Zoey-type ideas . . .

"Does it say when the bookstore's gonna start selling Stacy's backpacks?" Zoey asked. The gears in her head were turning. She had a plan and wanted to know when the best time would be to put it into action.

Nicole skimmed the article. "Yeah, it says Stacy's having some big meeting there this Friday."

Zoey nodded, starting to smile. "Interesting," she murmured.

"Ooooh, you're thinkin' things," Nicole said excitedly. This was the Zoey she knew.

Michael looked across the table at Zoey and nodded. She had that look. "Yeah, she's definitely thinkin' things," he agreed. And before long, Zoey would turn those thoughts into a plan.

Later that afternoon, Quinn was getting geared

up to battle the birds. She'd built a scarecrow — sort of. It actually looked more like a statue of herself with glowing red eyes, cool braids, and square glasses.

Crossing campus with his aching ears, Michael stopped in the courtyard to stare at the scarecrow as Quinn put the finishing touches on it. It looked pretty weird. He was tempted to just keep walking, but curiosity got the best of him. "Ummm, Quinn?" he asked hesitantly.

Quinn barely looked up from her work. She was busily adjusting the hip skirt and getting the scarecrow ready to stop any fowl play. "Hmmmmm?" she replied.

"What are you doing?" Michael asked. This had to be good — or at least totally freaky.

"Erecting a scarecrow to protect my b'napples from evil birds," Quinn said without even turning around. Wasn't it obvious? Wasn't it what anyone in her situation would do?

"Oh," Michael smirked, pointing at the scarecrow. "So that's supposed to scare them off?" It looked like Quinn had spent days working on her scarecrow — and while it was scary in a crazy kind of way for humans, he suspected it would make a great perch for birds to sit on while they chowed down on Quinn's b'napples.

"No," Quinn said simply.

Michael didn't get it. Wasn't a scarecrow supposed to scare birds away from a garden? "Then how does it protect your fruit?" he asked.

Quinn grinned. "Here, I'll show you," she offered. "Give me your hat."

Michael reached up and felt the brim of his purple baseball cap. It was new, and he really liked it. "Why?" he asked hesitantly.

Quinn didn't answer. Did he want to see how the scarecrow worked or not? It was one of her better — and bigger — Quinnventions, even if she did say so herself. "Give it to me," she repeated.

Feeling a little nervous, Michael handed over his cap.

"Now, watch what happens when your hat encroaches upon the fruit," Quinn instructed. She gleefully tossed the cap into the tree near a ripening bunch of b'napples. As soon as the cap came close to the fruit, red laser beams shot out of the scarecrow's eyes and zapped it. A second later, the cap landed on the ground, pierced, with smoke drifting out of the two quarter-size holes.

Michael picked up his cap and checked out the damage. His brand-new hat, ruined. "You know what?"

he said, as much to himself as to Quinn. "I should stop asking you so many questions." Shaking his head, he walked off with the smoldering hat. Then, after looking back over his shoulder at the statue and its crazy red eyes, he took off running.

CHAPTER 6

Backpack Payback

Wearing sunglasses and holding a *Cool Sunglasses* mag, Michael stood at his post in the PCA bookstore. He was working undercover and ready for action. Zoey had wasted no time in putting her plan into play. It had taken a team effort and a lot of work, but they were ready for Stacy's big meeting at the bookstore.

Just a few feet away, Stacy was talking with Marty, the bookstore manager, about her backpacks.

"So, I just expanded on my original idea and created these different styles," Stacy gushed, pointing to several backpacks laid out on the counter.

Marty looked over the packs and nodded with admiration. "Great. Just great," he said. "You know, kids come in here every day asking if we sell these."

Stacy beamed with pride. "Oh, really?" she asked.

"Yeah, and I'm always telling them, 'No, we don't sell Backpacks by Stacy.' But does that stop them? Nope." He folded his arms across his chest and nodded in a satisfied manner.

"Wow, that is so great." Stacy looked like she wanted to hug herself, the little thief. Michael couldn't wait to see her face when she found out about Zoey's plan.

"So, you ready to talk business?" Marty asked.

Stacy nodded. "I am. So all of these —" She pointed to all of her backpacks.

Michael couldn't wait another second. He lowered the magazine he was reading and pushed a button on his walkie-talkie.

"Zoey," he whispered. "The rabbit's in the hole."

The walkie-talkie crackled a little and then Michael heard Zoey's confused voice. "Huh? What rabbit?" she asked.

Michael rolled his eyes. Didn't the girl know a little code? Had she never watched a spy movie? Sheesh! "Stacy's here and the deal's goin' down!" he clarified quickly. He released the button. "And ya try to be cool," he murmured to himself, shouldering his backpack, shaking his head, and getting back to his surveillance.

Marty and Stacy had begun negotiating. Or were trying to, at least. They kept getting interrupted.

"Are these for sale yet?" a girl whined, pointing to the backpacks on the counter.

"Yeah," another kid chimed in. "When are they goin' on sale?"

Marty was used to reeling students in, but he had never seen such a frenzy over a product before. "Hey, hey!" he called loudly. "I'm trying to make a deal with the girl!"

One of the girls picked up a pack from the counter. "Girls, look how cool this is," she said, holding it up so everyone could see.

Stacy was thrilled. This could not have been going better. It was time to name her price. "Okay, I provide my backpacks, you sell them for seventy dollars apiece. Out of that, sixty-seven dollars goes to me and you get to keep —"

All of a sudden, Nicole burst into the store. "Hey, everybody!" she called excitedly, flashing a smile. "Come outside! You've gotta see this!"

Nicole turned and ran out as fast as she'd run in, and all the customers in the store followed.

Marty and Stacy stared after them. Stacy didn't look quite as smug as she had a moment before.

"Afternoon," Michael said casually as he headed out the door. This was going to be good.

"What's going on?" Marty asked. He definitely looked interested and took a few steps toward the door.

"Uh, I don't — I don't know," Stacy said as he started to leave. "Uh, sir! Sir!" She suddenly felt a little uncertain about things. Her customers were gone. Marty was gone. She wanted to nail down this deal, but she had no choice but to follow Marty out of the store.

When she got outside, Stacy's uncertainty turned to dread. She was staring at a very cool-looking booth full of very cool-looking backpacks. And Zoey was busily selling those backpacks to nearly every PCA student who passed by. She was so busy, she needed her friends to help her with all the sales!

"Okay, these are insane!" a girl named Annie said excitedly. She was holding one of Zoey's packs and looked practically giddy.

"Aren't they?" Dana agreed, giving the girl a high five and grinning.

It was payback time! And the look of shock on Stacy's face was priceless.

"So cool!" agreed a boy.

"I *so* gotta have one!" Kyle squealed.

Zoey stood under her BACKPACKS BY ZOEY sign, handing out backpacks, collecting money, and letting the whole thing sink in.

Marty leaned in toward Stacy. "What's all the fuss about?" he asked. The packs looked like Stacy's, but the kids were even more crazy about them.

"I-I don't know," Stacy admitted. As far as she could tell, the backpacks were like hers. But something was different. She felt her panic rise. She had to cut her deal with Marty before it was too late.

Marty left Stacy and stepped up to Zoey's stand to see for himself what the fuss was about.

"Hmmm? Eh — no, sir. That's the wrong way. Over here! Sir!" Stacy scrambled to get his attention — to get him back to the deal, *her* deal.

Marty smiled at Zoey. "Excuse me, what's going on here?" he asked.

Sitting in a tall director's chair next to her totally cool backpack booth, Zoey smiled and shrugged. "Oh, I'm just sellin' my backpacks," she said casually.

"Backpacks by Zoey," Nicole chimed in, in case that wasn't crystal clear. Zoey's plan was going great, and Nicole was thrilled to be a part of it. Payback was kickin'.

Just then Chase walked up to them, wearing one of Zoey's new packs. "Hey, Zoey, this feels awesome!" he congratulated her, wiggling his shoulders.

Marty eyed the backpack. "What does he mean, '*feels* awesome'?"

Nicole puffed up with pride over her roomie. She was more than happy to answer that. "Well, see, Zoey's backpacks have some cool new features," she explained.

Stacy scowled and stepped closer to Marty. She looked like she was getting desperate. "Sir, we were about to make a deal...." she said, gesturing to the school store.

Marty held up a hand. It was clear he wasn't going to let Stacy run the show. She could just hang on. "Wait." He turned back to Zoey and her friends. "What do you mean, 'cool new features'?"

Chase grinned. Obviously, Marty wanted more information. And he was in the right place! "Oh, y'see? You just turn this knob, and it massages your back." Chase turned it, and the backpack emitted a soft buzzing sound. "Oh, yeah, that's niiiice. That is tremendous." He really hammed it up, eyeing Stacy the whole time.

"You wanna try one?" Zoey offered, getting a backpack down off a hook and handing it to Nicole. Nicole slipped the backpack on Marty's back, and Nicole turned on the massager. The comforting buzzing sound echoed in the air.

"And then," Nicole prompted.

"Oh," Marty said, clearly surprised. "Oh-ho-ho-ho,

this feels good." He wiggled his shoulders like a hip-hop dancer.

Zoey and Nicole exchanged smiles.

Stacy was beginning to feel invisible. "Sir, our meeting?" she interrupted.

"And if you *really* want to relax, try the other knob." Nicole felt like she was on an infomercial, and loved it. Not only could she shop, she could *sell*.

Marty turned the other knob, and music played from tiny speakers on the backpack straps. "Oh, my God!" he exclaimed. "It's a radio, too?"

"Yes, sir," Zoey said proudly. It had been a lot of work getting these packs together so quickly, but the looks on the faces of her customers made it all worth it. This was one plan that was definitely paying off. "And you can plug your digital music player into it."

"So you can listen to music without having to stick headphones in your ears," Michael explained. His own ears were happy as clams since he'd gotten one of Zoey's new packs.

"Great!" Marty exclaimed. "Fantastic idea!"

"You're right," Chase agreed, looking over at Stacy. She looked like she had just swallowed something sour. "Just look around. People love 'em." He watched as Marty checked out the students walking by. They all had on

Backpacks by Zoey, and were all taking advantage of their great new features.

A girl named Jeanie wearing a Backpack by Stacy approached the stand. "Excuse me," she said. "I want to buy a Backpack by Zoey."

Stacy looked like she was about to throw up. "But you already have a Backpack by Stacy!" she objected.

"Yeah," Jeanie agreed. "But it's lame."

Stacy gasped. She was so shocked she looked like she was about to fall over. Zoey wasted no time. She handed Jeanie an orange-ish pack with full features. "How about this one?" she asked.

Jeanie took off her Backpack by Stacy and threw it aside. It flew through the air and landed in a large trash can.

Stacy gasped.

"I love this orange one! And it vibrates and plays music?" she asked.

"That's right," Zoey confirmed.

"I want it!" Jeanie said excitedly.

Marty looked around at all the Backpacks by Zoey that had already sold. "You're Zoey, right?" he asked.

"That's me," Zoey said proudly. She had had no idea how well her new ideas would pan out and was thrilled that everyone loved them so much.

"Listen, you want to make a deal — so we can sell your backpacks at the PCA bookstore?" he asked.

"Excuse me?!" Stacy huffed.

Marty ignored her and smiled at Zoey. "Come on, Zoey. We have a lot to talk about."

Zoey smiled at her friends as she and Marty walked back into the PCA store. This was awesome!

"Sir, wait!" Stacy called plaintively. "What about my backpacks?!"

Zoey couldn't resist. She turned back to Stacy. "Oh, there's one in the trash over there," she said sweetly.

Thanks to her second great idea, and some help from her friends, things were back on track.

Juke-tastic

Several days later, Zoey and her friends met up in the girls' lounge. Zoey had something she wanted to show them — something great.

"Okay, I know there's been a lot of questions about my backpack deal with the bookstore," she said.

Nicole smirked and shook her head. "No, not a lot of questions," she said meaningfully. There was really just one thing she was dying to know.

"Just one," Chase said, getting right to the point. "How much are you gonna make?"

Dana raised an eyebrow. "Yeah, how much cash are we talking here?" She personally hoped it was a lot. After all her hard work, Zoey deserved it. And maybe Zoey would buy some cool stuff for their dorm room.

"Hey, hey," Zoey said, raising her hands and trying to quiet everyone down. Nobody was listening. Finally,

Zoey whistled through her fingers — loudly. The room got very quiet very fast.

"Just so you know, I didn't take any money," she told everyone.

"Okay, um . . ." Chase wasn't sure how to break it to her. "That's a bad deal," he said, pointing a finger like a parent talking to a child.

"nooooo," Zoey promised. The deal she'd worked out was fine. In fact it was better than fine. It was awesome! "Instead of money, I asked for something cool. Something we could all use." She grinned and pointed to the big thing next to her that was covered with a sheet. Then, without further ado, she pulled the sheet off of it, revealing a very cool, very retro jukebox.

The kids went crazy. Everyone oohed and aahed.

"Look at that thing!" Dana exclaimed. It was the coolest jukebox she had ever seen.

"I know!" Zoey agreed. She had been thrilled when she'd thought of it. no more lame broken stereos in the lounge! She knew all the girls were going to love it. And the visiting guys wouldn't mind much, either.

Chase stared at the gleaming retro music machine. "Well, quit yappin' and juke it up!" he said.

Zoey pressed a button on the jukebox and the

CDs inside began to rotate. Then a second later, thumpin' music filled the room. "Isn't it cool?" she asked.

"Niiice," Chase said with an impressed nod. Another one of Zoey's great ideas.

"Beyond cool," Nicole said with an excited nod, and it was just like Zoey to share her profits with her friends in a such an awesome way.

Chase nodded again. "Yep, that is definitely juke-tastic." Everyone agreed as they stepped up to check out the new tune source.

Just then, Michael came into the lounge. "Hey," he greeted them, leaning on the side of the jukebox without even realizing what it was.

"Michael!" Zoey said. "Where ya been?"

"I was finishing up some homework," Michael explained. He usually liked to get it out of the way. "Hey, how come Quinn's all upset?"

Zoey had no idea, but knew she wanted to cheer her up. "Where is she?"

"Outside by her crazy tree," Michael said, shaking his head.

Chase and Zoey went out to find Quinn, leaving Michael alone. He stepped forward and noticed for the first time what he had been leaning on. His eyes bugged out as he stared at its shiny yellow finish and the zillions of CDs inside. "Man, that's juke-tastic!" he exclaimed, nodding to the beat.

Outside, Chase and Zoey found Quinn standing next to her tree. "Where did I go wrong?" she moaned, turning the b'napple over in her hand. She looked like she wanted to crawl into a cave.

"Hey, Quinn," Chase said with a wave.

"What's the matter?" Zoey asked.

"My b'napple tree stinks," Quinn replied flatly. She glanced up at the tree out of the corner of her eyes and got to her feet.

"Well, what's the problem with it?" Chase asked. He didn't really think he and Zoey could help, but maybe . . .

"I don't know," Quinn said sadly. "I guess something must have gone wrong when I combined the molecular structures."

Chase blinked. That wasn't exactly the explanation he was looking for.

"What, the b'napples don't taste good?" Zoey asked, trying to get an answer they could understand.

Thank you for translating, Chase thought.

"No," Quinn said. She had kissed that delicious b'napple flavor good-bye — forever. Her b'napples tasted bad, but it was worse than that. "They're dangerous," she added darkly.

"Dangerous?" Chase repeated. This could be interesting. "How?"

"Their juice is like a powerful acid," Quinn said. "Here, look." She carried a ripe b'napple over to the bike rack and squeezed some juice onto one of the bike seats. As the juice dribbled over the seat, it began to hiss and smoke. A few minutes later, what had been a bicycle seat was nothing more than a melted stump.

"Back to square one," Quinn said with a sad sigh. Zoey put her arm around her friend and led her away. You win some, you lose some. Chase followed. As they rounded a corner, Stacy approached the bike with the melted seat. When she saw the goopy, plastic mess, her eyes widened in horror. "My bike!" she wailed.

Later that day, Zoey, Chase, Nicole, Michael, and Dana were all heading to class together — and sporting Zoey's new backpacks.

"Hey, love the backpack, Zoey!" Kyle said, stopping her on the path.

"You're a genius!" a boy agreed, slinging his own pack onto his back.

"Thanks!" Zoey said. It was totally awesome to have her packs on the backs of so many PCA students. And everyone seemed to love them!

"You did good, Zo'," Chase complimented, smiling at his friend.

"Yeah, she did," Nicole agreed with a nod.

Just then, Stacy rode by them on her bike, talking to herself. "Ow, ow, ow, ow," she cried out, wincing at every tiny bump on her unpadded seat.

Zoey smiled to herself. *Nice work, Quinn,* she thought. The b'napples were good for something after all.

CHAPTER 8

Stressing Out

Zoey strolled across the manicured campus of Pacific Coast Academy, trying to clear her head. Facts and figures were bouncing around her brain like balls in a pinball machine. It was hard-core cram time at PCA. All over campus, kids were biting their nails and burying their heads in their books. Even Zoey was feeling the pressure. She was so wrapped up in exam stress she barely noticed the sun on her shoulders or the ocean breeze in her blond hair.

She needed to relax. After all that hard work on the backpacks she'd been making and selling, she didn't want to get herself all stressed out. Zoey took a deep breath. She had studied hard all term. If she could hit the books just a little bit today she should be okay. It was everyone else she was worried about.

"Hey, Zoey." Karen, a fellow PCA upperclassman

rushed up to Zo' looking totally intense. "I have my English exam tomorrow morning," she said with a hand on Zoey's shoulder. "Can I borrow your notes? Mine are lame." Karen had a pleading look in her eyes.

"Sure. Come on by my dorm and pick them up later. Room 101." Zoey smiled. She loved that her dorm room number sounded like an introductory college course.

"Thanks! *Ciao!*" Karen said, sounding relieved. Zoey's notes were always good.

As Karen hurried away, Zoey spotted Mark. He looked even more freaked out than Karen had.

"Hey, Mark. How'd your history exam go?" Zoey asked.

Mark looked at her wide-eyed for a second. His broad face seemed to crack. His eyes filled with tears, his chin quivered, and he let out a sob before burying his face in his hands, turning and running away.

"Better luck next semester!" Zoey called after him. Maybe she shouldn't have asked.

Heaving a sigh, Zoey slung her pack off and stashed it under a table next to the campus coffee cart. Then she took a load off, pulled out her laptop, opened her e-mail, and started to type:

Dear Mom and Dad,
Well, my first semester at PCA is almost over. It's been awesome, but now we have exams so everyone's like freakin' out — especially me 'cause all my friends keep asking me to help them study. First I had to help Nicole with history. . . .

Just thinking about their study session made Zoey cringe. Nicole was smart, but she had sort of a one-track mind.

"So, President Lincoln was assassinated by Gerald Ford while sitting in a booth." Even after they had studied for an hour, Nicole still had it all mixed up.

"Nooo." Zoey had tried really hard to be patient. But it hadn't been easy. "Lincoln was assassinated by John Wilkes Booth at Ford's Theater," she'd explained *again.*

"Hey, you know who's cute?" Nicole's mind had spun back onto her favorite subject — boys. "Ricky Ford," she cooed. "He's in my theater class, and he has really great hair." Twirling the pink pencil that matched her outfit, she had nodded and raised her eyebrows like she was reporting some amazing fact.

"Uh-huh." Nicole kept nodding at Zoey like her friend had been unable to fathom the big hair news. But what Zoey could not understand was how Nicole managed to stay at PCA when her mind was always on guys and *not* her classes.

Shaking the memory out of her mind, Zoey kept typing:

... Then I had to help Michael study for his algebra exam. ...

Pausing for a second, Zoey remembered that fiasco. It had not gone much better than Nicole's study sesh.

"Wait, tell me the quadratic formula one more time?" Michael had asked.

"X equals negative B, plus or minus the square root of B, minus four A C over two A," Zoey told him slowly for the bazillionth time.

Michael had let that sink in for a second. Zoey hoped he might actually have been getting it. Finally.

"Okay," Michael had said slowly, "now, tell me the quadratic formula one more time?"

After Michael, there had been Quinn. She was amazing with science, but French was like, well, a foreign language to her.

"Okay, *omelette du fromage* means ..." Zoey had prompted her.

"Cheese omelet?" Quinn had squeaked.

"Right!" Zoey had been glad that at last someone was getting the *answers* right! But some of Quinn's *questions* . . .

"Okay, now how would I say, 'I melted my father's sports car'?" Quinn had asked.

At that point it might have been best to let Quinn study alone. But Zoey had not been able to help herself. "Why?" she'd asked. Why would anyone need to say they had melted a car in French — or in any language, for that matter?

"I did that," Quinn had confessed quietly.

And that wasn't all. Zoey kept typing to her parents.

. . . Then Logan asked me to help him get ready for his English exam. . . .

She was not sure how she had gotten roped into helping Logan with poetry, but it had not been pretty.

"Remember," she'd told him, "a haiku is a poem with three lines: five syllables, then seven syllables, and then five syllables. And they don't rhyme. Now give it a try."

"Okay, umm . . ." Logan had paused for a moment,

letting the wind ruffle his curls. Then, with his hand on his chest, he'd recited his poem like he was reading Shakespeare.

Always optimistic, Zoey had hoped for the best. But what she'd gotten was nothing but an earful of ego.

"Handsome guy, I am. Everyone knows I am hot. Girls want to kiss me." When Logan had finished with a flourish of raised eyebrows and the smuggest look ever, he turned to Zoey like she should applaud or something. "How was that?" he had asked.

Zoey's stomach lurched just thinking about it. "Nauseating," she'd told him.

Anyway, the good news is . . .

Zoey was about to wrap up her letter to her parents when she saw a familiar pair of shoes stop at her table.

"Hey, Zo'." It was Chase. He had his pack slung on one shoulder, an open blue shirt over a red T-shirt, and a funny look on his face. "Listen, I got my biology exam this afternoon," he said a little sheepishly, "so would you help me go over the whole recessive/dominant gene thing?"

With a sigh and a half-smile, Zoey nodded. "Sure. Sit."

She closed her laptop and set it aside. It was study time *again*. "Okay. I have brown eyes, right?" Zoey started slowly. Hopefully, they would only have to go over this once.

"Right," Chase agreed. Couldn't argue with that. Zoey's eyes were the color of chocolate, and Chase loved any excuse to look into them.

"That's a dominant gene," Zoey explained. "You have green eyes," she went on.

"Okay." This wasn't so hard. Brown eyes. Green eyes. Chase had it so far.

"That's a recessive gene," Zoey said.

"Okay." Chase nodded again. Brown, dominant. Green, recessive.

"So, if we ever got married and had a baby, there's a seventy-five percent chance he'd have brown eyes, and a twenty-five percent chance he'd have green eyes," Zoey explained.

Hang on. Chase was lost. He had it a second ago, but there was something he could not get past. "Are you asking me to marry you?" He pointed at Zoey.

Zoey sighed. "You wanna be serious?" she asked,

getting a little exasperated. She was willing to help, but if Chase was just going to waste her time . . .

"Okay, okay." Chase surrendered with his hands up. "Brown eyes are dominant, and green eyes are recessive —"

"Hey, Zoey." Right behind their table, John was getting a latte at the coffee cart. He spotted Chase and Zoey studying. It looked like a good idea. "Later on, would you help me study for my chemistry exam?" he asked Zoey casually.

Zoey could not believe her ears. She threw her hands up and screamed in frustration. Chase and John looked shocked.

"Okay." John picked up his cup and backed away slowly. "I'll ask someone else."

When John was gone, Chase leaned across the table. "Little tense, are you?" It was almost impossible not to pick up on *that* vibe.

Zoey was trying hard not to lose it, but the situation was getting ridiculous. "Well, everyone keeps asking me to help them study," she said, "and I wanna be nice, but I have my own exams, too, ya know, and it's not like anyone offers to help me study, and I just don't —"

Chase's eyes were getting bigger and bigger as Zoey's voice got louder and louder. She was so upset, the dorm room key she always wore around her neck so she wouldn't lose it was bouncing wildly on her chest and her cheeks were turning red.

"All right, all right, shhhhh." Chase spoke in a soothing voice to try to get her off her rant. "Caaaalm down. Exams are over tomorrow morning and then we get to go to the best party, like, ever," he reminded her about the end-of-semester beach party.

Zoey had never been before, but she had heard stories. And nothing made her feel better than the beach — except maybe a party on the beach. "It's really awesome?" she asked, letting the memory of all the studying fade into the background.

"The best," Chase assured her. "Mystic Beach is incredible. We get to play volleyball, go boogie-boarding, we have this big cookout —" Chase ticked off on his fingers all of the fabulous things there were to do.

"Hey, Zoey. Chase. What's going on?" Mr. Bender greeted them, leaning on the coffee cart, holding a fat wad of papers in his hand.

Chase waved. Zoey smiled and waved, too. Mr. Bender was cool for a teacher. "What's doin'?" Chase asked.

"Grading exams." Mr. Bender shrugged, grabbing his coffee. "I've already gone through, like, nine red pens." He rolled his eyes. Exams were rough on everyone at PCA.

"Yikes." Chase flinched. He hoped Mr. Bender hadn't gone through too much red ink on *his* exam.

Mr. Bender was about to walk away when a strange sound started emanating from his bag. It was like an alien alarm clock or something.

"What is that?" Zoey asked.

"Oh!" Mr. Bender's face lit up as he pulled a small silver phone out of his messenger bag. "That's my new cell phone," he explained.

"Cool ringtone." Chase's phone played one of those tunes you could never get out of your head once it was in.

"Thanks." Mr. Bender flipped the phone open. "It gets even cooler! It's got two-way visual calling."

Mr. Bender's wife appeared on the screen holding a small piece of clothing and waving it back and forth on the screen. "David, you left your underwear on the floor again," she scolded him.

"Uhhh, gotta call you back." Mr. Bender quickly snapped the phone shut and shuffled away to the tune of Chase's and Zoey's stifled laughter.

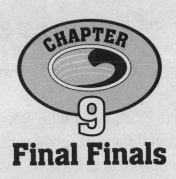

CHAPTER 9

Final Finals

"All right, students, Exam Week is officially over!" The teacher at the front of the room was drowned out by cheering PCA students. Zoey, Nicole, and Dana gathered their things while Chase and Michael high-fived in the back of the classroom.

Most of the students filed out of the room, leaving their papers on the teacher's desk as a blond, mop-topped underclassman in swim trunks came in the classroom.

"Zoey! Hey!" Zoey's little brother, Dustin, plopped down on a chair. He had a beach towel slung over his shoulder and his brown eyes were sparkling.

"Hey!" Zoey shot back. "Look at you in your cute swimsuit."

"Thanks." Dustin shrugged off Zoey's compliment. She was always calling him cute. "Um, would it be okay if

I rode down to the beach in your bus?" he asked. Zoey's friends were all hanging around her desk. Dustin hoped she would not think he was too little or in the way.

"Yeah, sure, if it's okay with your teacher." Zoey shrugged. She didn't see why not and she kind of liked hanging out with her little brother.

Dustin grinned.

Just then Quinn rushed in wearing yellow pants and a blue tie-dyed poncho over a tank top. She was holding a vial of creamy white stuff. "Okay, people! You gotta check this out!" she bubbled.

Zoey sat back. She had seen too many of Quinn's experiments and inventions to look too closely. In fact, her ears were still ringing just a tiny bit from the sonic device Quinn created to get revenge on the guys during Prank Week.

"Uh-oh. What now?" Michael looked positively freaked; he hadn't gotten over the loss of his hat to Quinn's b'napple scarecrow. Dana, Logan, and Nicole looked nervous, too.

"You're not going to blow us up, are you?" Chase asked nervously.

"Noooo." Quinn shook her head. "Though I could," she said more thoughtfully, letting her mind wander.

Suddenly, she snapped back to the task at hand. "Anyway, I finished my chemistry exam in like ten minutes, so since I had some extra time, I combined a few chemicals and accidentally created an aroma that smells exactly like coconut!"

"Coooool," Logan said sarcastically. "But no one cares," he snarled. Logan had not quite gotten over being knocked out cold on the lawn by Quinn's last experiment. It had totally messed up his hair.

"Oh, come on. Just sniff it." Quinn pulled out the rubber stopper and held the vial in front of Dustin's nose. He breathed in deeply. Then she waved the test tube in front of Zoey, Nicole, Dana, Michael, Chase, and Logan, letting them each catch a whiff. A soft white wisp wafted into their noses.

"Wow," Nicole said, sounding a little shocked. "That really does smell like coconut."

Zoey nodded. It smelled good. And the smell of coconut couldn't do too much damage, could it?

"I know, isn't it cool?" Quinn was practically bouncing off the walls, she was so giddy with her latest creation. She breathed the scent in deeply.

Zoey yawned. Then Nicole yawned. Then Dana. The yawn made its way through the crowd in that infectious way yawns do.

"Man," Michael stretched his arms over his head. "I feel like taking a nap."

"What?" Chase covered his mouth to keep people from seeing his tonsils while he yawned. "We can't sleep. We gotta . . ." His voice trailed off. He forgot what he was going to say. All he wanted was to find a pillow big enough to lie down on. "We gotta . . ."

If Chase had been able to finish his sentence, there would not have been anyone awake to hear it. Zoey and Logan slumped across their desks, asleep. Chase dropped back into a chair. Dana, Nicole, Michael, Dustin, and Quinn collapsed into piles on the floor with a *whump*. And soon, the only sound in the room was the heavy breathing of deep sleepers.

Michael's cell phone rang. He struggled up from the floor and fished it out of his pocket. "Hello?" he said groggily. "No. This isn't Achmed. Wrong number." Michael staggered a bit, trying to get his bearings. Where was he? What time was it? He looked at the clock on his cell. "Eleven forty-five?!" Their last exam ended at ten! They had lost almost two hours. "Zoey! Chase! Logan! Dana! Wake up!" Michael shouted. He shook his friends to try and rouse them. Slowly, they came out of their stupor and sat up. Dana, Nicole, and Quinn stood up from the floor.

Zoey and Logan sat up and stretched. "What happened?" Zoey asked, blinking. She felt really out of it.

"We all fell asleep!" Michael explained.

"It must be an effect of my synthetic coconut aroma." Quinn nodded, adding, "That's weird."

"So are you!" Logan looked at the dark-haired science geek like she was an exhibit in the zoo. Quinn glared back.

"What time is it?" Zoey asked, looking around.

"Eleven forty-six!" Michael shouted. Why weren't they getting this? They had been asleep almost two hours — two hours of beach time!

"What?! The last bus for Mystic Beach leaves at noon!" Chase yelled, finally getting it.

Nicole looked panicked. "How are we gonna get there in fourteen minutes?!" she asked. It took her longer than that just to de-frizz her hair!

"We have to! C'mon!" Zoey jumped up and grabbed her bag. "Go! Go! Go! Go! Go!" Everyone raced out of the room. Well, almost everyone.

Zoey turned back, followed by Quinn and Chase. Dustin was still passed out cold lying across one of the desks.

"Dustin! Dustin, wake up! C'mon!" Zoey shook her brother. He did not respond.

"Why's he still sleeping?" Zoey asked Quinn. The rest of them had woken up.

"Probably because he's younger and smaller, so it'll take a little while for the effects to wear off." Quinn said. She hoped her theory was right.

"Well, that's very nice, but we don't have time for that!" Zoey threw up her hands. They needed Dustin to wake up *now*! They could not just leave him here, but they had to catch that bus!

"I'll take him!" Chase said. He grabbed the younger kid and heaved him up on one shoulder. Dustin flopped there like a caught fish — a really, really big fish.

Zoey smiled at Chase gratefully. "We're gonna get our stuff and meet you at the bus!" she said as they raced out of the room.

"Right!" Chase called back.

The whole crew hauled their cabooses to their dorms as quickly as they could. They had to get their gear and get back on track. Chase ran full tilt with Dustin bouncing up and down on his shoulders, snoring softly.

Zoey felt like she was in a mad dash as she rounded the corner and started down the steps to the bus stop. She, Nicole, Quinn, and Dana were dressed in their beach gear and carrying towels and bags and beach balls — all the necessary supplies they could grab in two seconds.

From the other direction Logan, Michael, and Chase, with Dustin in tow, came running just as fast. The groups merged and sprinted down the steps toward the PCA bus sitting on the curb. It was loaded with kids anxious to get to the party.

Zoey and her friends had made it just in time — to see the doors close and the bus pull away.

"Wait!"

"Stop!"

"Wait for us!"

They all yelled and ran, but it was no use. The driver did not see them, and he couldn't hear them over the cheers of the passengers.

"Well, what are we gonna do now?" Nicole panted. She hated to think she had gotten all dressed up in her new board shorts and tank for nothing.

"Can't someone else take us?" Dana asked.

"That was the last bus." Zoey sighed, letting her shoulders slump. She felt like a deflated beach ball.

"Man, the whole school's on their way to Mystic Beach." Chase tried not to whine. But it was hard to feel upbeat with a kid on your shoulder.

Logan was the only one who seemed unfazed. "We'll just call a cab," he said, like it was that simple.

"A cab?" Nicole looked at Logan like his head was spinning around and flames were shooting out of his mouth. "Mystic Beach is, like, fifty-five miles from here!"

"You wanna know what a cab would cost?" Zoey asked. It would probably total more than her lifetime birthday money savings.

"Oh." Logan's voice was dripping with mock disappointment. "If only we knew somebody with a very rich daddy, and . . ." While he talked, Logan slid his wallet out and withdrew a slim piece of platinum-colored plastic. "His very rich daddy's credit card." He waved the credit card in the air.

Nicole's eyes were so big Zoey thought they might pop out. Logan was full of surprises. For about a second, Zoey thought she should tell Logan to put it away. They should not spend Logan's dad's money on a cab. Then she remembered how stressed out she had been and how much she was looking forward to a little fun in the sun.

"Cell phone, please." Logan pushed past Zoey and Nicole and held out his hand. Michael slapped his cell into Logan's palm. Logan dialed and held the phone to his ear. "Relax, children," he said condescendingly. "We'll be at that party in no time."

The yellow minivan cab pulled to a stop by the plant-covered dunes. Logan signed the cab bill, and the rest of the crew piled out onto the sand. With excited cries, they raced down the path toward the water's edge.

"All right! Yeah!" Chase still had a snoozing Dustin on his shoulder. But it could not dampen his mood now. They'd finally made it.

"Whoo! We're here!" Quinn shouted.

"Mystic Beach, here we come!" Michael looked around for a place to stake his umbrella.

"Yes!" Logan nodded, triumphant.

Zoey scanned the beach. It was huge. It was gorgeous. It was hot and sandy and completely deserted. "Okay, where is everybody?" she asked.

"Maybe we're the first ones here?" Dana suggested hopefully. Something was seriously wrong.

"No, we left after everyone else," Chase reminded them. There was no way they could have gotten to Mystic ahead of the others.

"Then where's the PCA party?" Michael asked the question they all wanted an answer to.

"Oh, hey, I think the kid's starting to wake up." Dustin was starting to stir. Chase put him down on the sand gently.

"Uh, where am I?" Dustin asked, looking around confusedly. He was still groggy.

"We're at Mystic Beach," Zoey told him.

Dustin turned all the way around, taking in the sun and the wind and the waves and the sand. "Where is everybody?" he asked.

"We're trying to figure that out." Michael raised his eyebrows. He didn't want to be the first one to say it, but he suspected that Logan had messed something up.

Zoey looked at Logan. "Are you sure you gave the cab driver the right directions?" she asked.

"Yes." Logan looked sure of himself. But then, he always looked sure of himself. "I looked it up on the Net. Mystic Beach is exactly fifty-seven miles north of PCA."

"No, it's not." Dustin shook his head. "Mystic Beach is *south* of PCA."

"Dustin, are you sure?" Zoey asked. Everyone was staring at her little brother. He was pretty smart, but Logan *had been* the one to look it up.

"Who are you gonna trust?" Dustin asked. "Me or pretty boy?" He waved his arm in Logan's direction.

"Look, you little kid —" Logan started to go after

Dustin, but Chase stepped in and put a protective arm around the younger guy.

"Hey, don't yell at him, all right? This is your fault!" Chase yelled. Dana slapped the back of Logan's head, and Chase went on losing it. "Now we're two hours away from the party, stuck in the middle of nowhere on a deserted beach, and I'm extremely sad about it!" Chase was totally freaking. He looked like he might even cry.

"Will you chill?" Logan sneered, crossing his arms across his chest.

"Not really!" Chase shouted back.

"Guys. Let's not get upset." Zoey's voice was calm. She was cool. She could handle this — they all could. "We have our cell phones," she said reasonably. "We'll just call someone and get a ride."

Everyone relaxed a little. "The girl says good things." Michael grinned. They could have their fun yet. Everyone reached for their phones.

Chase peered at the tiny screen. "Uh-oh. I got no signal here. Zo'?"

"No bars." Zoey shrugged. She turned to Dana. "You got bars?"

Dana and Michael both shook their heads.

"No service," Michael confirmed.

"Well, this is just great." Chase smiled, but his tone was sarcastic.

"Come on!" Ever the cheerleader, Nicole tried to rally the crowd. "I'm sure Zoey's got a plan here." Nicole smiled at Zoey hopefully. Zoey always had a plan. Didn't she? "Whatcha thinkin', Zo'?" she prompted her.

"Well . . ." Zoey tried to keep the panic out of her voice. Why was everyone looking at her? She didn't get them into this mess, and she had no idea how to get them out of it! "I'm thinkin' we're two hours away from the party, stuck in the middle of nowhere on a deserted beach, and I'm extremely sad about it!"

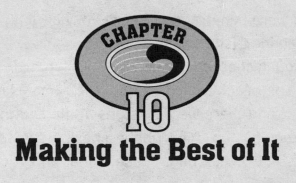

Making the Best of It

Nicole's feet felt like lead as she plodded through the sand, carrying all her beach stuff. The sun was beating down on them, and they'd been walking for what seemed like forever! "Okay, I gotta rest," she announced, dropping the beach ball, her bag and towel, and herself onto the sand. She could not go another step.

"Me, too," Dustin said, practically collapsing beside her.

Zoey nodded. "Okay, let's sit down for a sec." How long had they been walking, anyway? Too long, as far as she was concerned.

Quinn dropped to the sand. She was so tired she was losing interest in using this experience as a science experiment. She didn't even care how quickly water was evaporating from their bodies or how quickly the sun's

UV rays were penetrating their skin! "How long have we been walking?" she groaned.

Logan checked his watch. "Over an hour," he said grimly. The beach looked exactly the same as it had an hour ago, and there were no signs of life anywhere.

Zoey sat up. "Cell phone check," she said, pulling hers out of her bag. Chase, Dana, and Michael did the same.

"No bars," Michael said forlornly. His purple T-shirt was damp and clinging to his back.

"None," Dana agreed with a grimace.

"Not a bar," Chase added, shaking his dark curly head.

Zoey sighed and shoved her phone back into her beach bag. "So now what do we do?" she asked.

"Keep walkin'?" Michael suggested. It was lame, but the best he could think of.

Nicole looked dismayed. They were stranded on the beach and had no idea where they were! "Why?" she said hopelessly. "We don't even know if we're walking in the right direction!"

"We should just stay put and wait for someone to come along and find us," Quinn said reasonably.

Zoey didn't have anything better to offer. "Okay," she agreed, getting to her feet and brushing the sand off her clothes. "But I'm gonna look around a little bit."

"Look for what?" Logan asked skeptically.

Zoey rolled her eyes — couldn't he see the bright side for half a second? Sitting around complaining was not going to do any of them any good. "I don't know," she said with a shrug. "A pay phone, a person, maybe a coconut to hit someone with for getting us into this!" she said, raising an eyebrow.

Logan refused to admit that this situation was his fault. How was he to know there were two Mystic Beaches! "Hey, if it wasn't for me we'd all be stuck back at school," he insisted, ignoring the fact that there was a beach across the street from school, and it was a lot closer to the cafeteria and everything else they might need.

Nicole glared at him. "You mean where there's buildings and air-conditioning and cell phone reception?" she said pointedly.

Chase held up his hands. "Okay, okay," he said, trying to play peacemaker. Things were bad enough without everyone fighting. "Let's not argue. Just look around and see what we can find."

Everyone got to their feet and spread out to look around. The beach was pretty clean, but it was worth a shot. Besides, what else were they gonna do?

Fifteen minutes later, Michael dumped a big inner tube on the sand at his friends' feet. "I found an inner tube," he announced. He had no idea what they could do with it, but it was something.

Dana tossed a bunch of tangled rope on top of the tube. "I found some old rope," she said with a shrug.

"I found a broken old fishing pole," Zoey chimed in, tossing it onto the pile.

"I found sand," Chase mumbled. He sprinkled a handful onto the found goods.

Nicole felt like she was going to cry. "Okay, this is officially horrible!" she wailed. "After a whole week of exams, this is our day of fun?" It was too awful to be true.

"I know," Chase agreed. "And, like, somewhere two hours away from here, every student at PCA is whoopin' it up and" — he waved his arms in frustration and scowled — "we're not."

Michael looked around miserably. "I was supposed to be boogie-boardin' right now." He gestured to the ocean frustratingly. "There's no boogie here."

Dustin sighed sadly. "You're lucky. I was dragged here unconscious." He shot Quinn a look.

"You weren't unconscious. You were sleeping invol-untarily," Quinn corrected, her crocheted poncho flapping in the breeze. It really bugged her when people used scientific terminology incorrectly.

"Whatever," Dustin said. The point was, he did not come here of his own free will.

"This is such a nightmarish way to end the semester," Nicole grumbled, folding her arms across her green mesh cover-up.

"Totally," Quinn agreed.

"I know," Chase said with a nod.

Everyone joined in the whining until it was a big pity party. Zoey looked around at her friends. They were wallowing in their own misery! What was so terrible about being on the beach with your best pals? Nothing, as long as everyone was looking at it that way. What everyone needed was a new perspective.

"C'mon, guys!" Zoey said, sounding a little like a cheerleader. "We worked our butts off on those exams!" They deserved a little celebration, and they could give it to themselves!

"Yeah, we did," Chase agreed, not getting Zoey's point. Why rub it in?

"And we came here to party on the beach, right?"

"Yeah!" everyone chorused, starting to get the message.

"Okay, then." Zoey got down to the details. "Michael and Dana, you got music, right?"

Michael and Dana nodded together. They were both into their tunes. "Yup," Michael confirmed with a grin. He never went anywhere without his music, and Dana rarely did, either.

"All right, then!" Zoey cheered. "Let's crank up some music and quit bein' a bunch of lame losers!"

"Yeah!" Chase agreed, clapping his hands together.

Michael pumped a fist in the air. "Let's shake up this beach and get this party started!" he shouted.

Everyone let out a whoop and a cheer while Michael plugged his Mp3 player into Dana's boom box. He cranked it up, and surf music filled the air.

"How about some football?" Chase asked, pulling an orange ball from his green camo backpack. It was four against four, and Zoey scored a touchdown before anyone could stop her. Then Logan made it into the end zone to even the score, and Dustin caught a ride on Michael's back and went all the way.

"Limbo!" Nicole called out excitedly. She loved parties and party games! They took turns holding the old fishing pole and, one by one, wiggled their way under it while they cheered one another on. All except Michael. He flipped the pole up and walked right through.

Next, they held a sand castle competition. Dana went for a kind of Egyptian pyramid look. Michael built a small castle on a kind of ridge. But Quinn built an entire castle village, complete with a bridge and moats and several perfectly formed buildings.

They were having tons of fun and up next it was tug-o-war time. With waves crashing over their feet and legs, Dustin, Zoey, Chase, and Michael squared off against Dana, Logan, Nicole, and Quinn. It was an even match, with both sides pulling hard. Then Zoey's team let go of the rope, sending the other team into the waves. Laughing, they came up sputtering and lunged for the other team. There were tackles all around. All bets were off. But there were no losers.

"Woo-hoo!" Zoey cheered as she fell into a whitecap. She was having a blast, and by the looks of things, so were her friends.

"Inner tube rides!" Michael said, running onto the beach and grabbing the tube he'd found. He tied the old rope around it and the guys took turns pulling the girls — and Dustin.

The beach party had started out a total downer, Dana thought as she crashed through the waves on the tube, but was turning out to be a great time. As she followed her friends out of the water and onto the beach, she realized she had to hand it to Zoey for getting them out of their funk.

Exhausted but happy, the kids plopped down on the warm sand.

"Yeah!" Nicole said, wiped out but psyched. They'd really managed to turn the afternoon around.

"Awesome!" Chase put in. It may not be Mystic Beach, but spending the day on any beach with his friends — especially Zoey — was proving to be a great time.

When the Party's Over

"That was so much fun!" Quinn flopped down on the sand, her funky ponytails bobbing. Everyone agreed. Their private beach party was turning out great. But they were starting to get worn out and there were a few cold hard facts they had to face. The group of friends looked around at one another in silence.

Finally, Chase spoke. "You know, guys, I hate to be a downer, but we are still stuck out here."

Zoey sighed. As much as she hated to admit it, Chase had a point. She checked her phone one more time. Nothing. "I wish our stupid cell phones would work," she grumbled.

"Hey, you know?" Michael said, remembering. "I totally forgot — I have my laptop in my book bag."

Chase's eyes lit up. "Oh, you serious, dude?" he asked. "Go get it!"

Michael pushed himself up off the sand and ran over to his bag.

"Wait. Why do we need his computer?" Dana asked. She didn't see how it could help.

"Because if we can pick up a network, we can instant-message someone to come find us and get us out of here," Chase explained.

Logan shot Chase a "duh" look. "Dude, if our cell phones don't get reception, what makes you think we'll be able to IM?" he pointed out a little smugly.

Chase scowled at his roommate. Why was Logan always so negative? "You got a better idea?" he asked.

Zoey rolled her eyes at the guys. All this bickering was getting on her nerves. She got to her feet and walked toward the ocean. Dustin was still hanging out in the water — he had been there practically the whole party!

"Hey, Dustin!" she called. "Come out of the water! You're gonna shrivel up like a prune!"

Dustin stood in chest-high water. He shook his head firmly. "No! I'm not comin' out!" he insisted.

Zoey didn't get it. "Why not?" she asked.

"A big wave pulled off my bathing suit!" he confessed.

"Well, where is it?" Zoey asked the obvious question.

Dustin grimaced. "If I knew, I wouldn't be hanging out in the water!"

Behind her, Zoey's friends were chuckling to themselves as they considered Dustin's predicament. Zoey shot them a look. They weren't helping!

"Look, you're gonna have to come out eventually!" she said.

Dustin shook his head firmly. "I'll come out when you find me some pants!" he shouted over the waves.

As much as she hated to admit it, Zoey had to give up — at least for the moment. Dustin was not coming out.

Behind her, Michael was fiddling with his open laptop.

"You getting a signal?" Nicole asked hopefully.

Michael shook his head and wiggled a little. "No," he admitted. "But I figured something out. If you turn it like —"

All of a sudden, Quinn let out a bloodcurdling scream. Everyone jumped.

"What?!" Zoey asked, her heart pounding in her chest. She was used to Nicole screaming like that, but not Quinn.

"I have an idea," Quinn said calmly.

"Is it about how to restart my heart?" Chase asked, still jolted. He felt like he'd just suffered a minor heart attack.

"No," Quinn replied casually. "But if you let me use your laptop and one of you guys lets me use your cell phone, I can combine the circuits and boost the RF output with the computer's battery." She grinned like an inventor who had just completed a perfect prototype.

Logan looked at Quinn over the tops of his rectangular sunglass frames. He had no idea what she had just said, and wasn't sure he really wanted to. "And that means?" he asked, waving his hand in the air.

"I can probably triple the cell phone's range so we can make a phone call!" she exclaimed happily.

"Awesome!" Nicole said. As weird as Quinn was, her scientific knowledge was impressive — and helpful — if it didn't put them to sleep!

"But I don't want you tearing apart my laptop," Michael objected. She had ruined his new baseball cap just a few weeks ago!

Chase gazed lovingly at his cell phone through his curly bangs. "This cell phone is like my child!" he said, stroking it like a baby's head.

Zoey gave Chase an "oh, please" look. "Do you

want to stay here tonight and freeze to death?" Zoey knew it probably wasn't cold enough to actually freeze anything, but the ocean air did get seriously chilly at night.

With a sigh, both Chase and Michael handed over their goods. Quinn accepted them eagerly. "This shouldn't take long," she said.

Chase shook his head. "Y'know, even if Quinn can make that work, it's still gonna be a long time before someone comes and gets us." His stomach was growling, and he could feel the temperature dropping a bit. How long would they be here?

"Yeah," Logan agreed. "And I'm starving."

Nicole nodded, pulling her knees up to her chest. "Yeah, me, too," she agreed.

Zoey smiled and got to her feet. It was time to take action once again. Besides, she had an idea. "Come on, Logan, Chase," she ordered. "Let's go catch a fish."

Logan rolled his eyes. Sometimes girls were so forgetful. "And what are we supposed to use for bait?" he asked.

Nicole smirked. "You're a boy," she teased. "Go dig up some worms."

Logan made a face. "Gross!" he said.

Zoey shook her head. For a tough guy, Logan sure

was a wimp. "C'mon, I'll protect you from the worms," she teased, resting the fishing pole on her shoulders.

"Wait!" Michael called after the fishing trio. "What are we supposed to do?"

"Build a fire!" Zoey called back. That should keep them busy for a while.

"How!?" Nicole was confused. There was no stack of split firewood, no fireplace, and no matches!

Zoey turned back to her friends. "Figure it out!" she challenged and walked away.

Michael stared after her. Then he turned to the girls standing next to him. "You guys build that fire," he said. He lay down on the sand and stretched out to get comfortable, exposing his chocolate-brown skin to the sun. "I'm gonna be working on my tan." He put his hands behind his head and closed his eyes behind his shades.

Nicole and Dana exchanged looks. There was *no way* Michael was getting out of this one. Building a fire was going to take major teamwork. All at once they grabbed him by the wrists and pulled him to his feet.

Nearby, Quinn sat on a blanket working on her communications experiment. She used her pocketknife to open the back of the computer, then unscrewed the back of the phone. She pulled several wires out of each one and used her knife to strip away the plastic coating.

She smiled as she worked. Who would have guessed that a beach party could be this much fun!

Nicole combed the beach looking for firewood. But all of the pieces were huge! She, Dana, and Michael each dragged a big piece across the sand and put them into a pile. Then they found more and more. Pretty soon they were looking at a big pile of driftwood.

"Nice work!" Nicole said.

Dana gave a satisfied nod. They had definitely gathered a lot of wood.

Zoey, Chase, and Logan were busily digging up worms. Well, Zoey and Chase were. Logan just sort of pawed at the sand like a little kid. Zoey didn't get it. What was the big deal? She dug deep into the sand with her hands. A second later she pulled out a really big worm and waved it in front of Logan's face.

"Whoa!" Logan said, scrambling backward across the sand like an awkward crab.

In the ocean, Dustin watched the bigger kids working. He kind of wanted to help, but mostly he was bored. He'd been in here for, like, four hours, and was getting cold — not to mention pruny.

Chase raised the fishing pole above his head and pressed the lever near the handle. The line flew out into the ocean, nearly hitting Dustin's head.

"Hey!" Dustin protested.

Zoey giggled. They weren't professional fishers, that was for sure. But the line was out there with the fish in the sea.

All of a sudden, there was a tug on the end of the line. They had something! Logan reeled it in. But as soon as it was out of the water Zoey could tell it wasn't your typical fish. For one thing, it was red. For another, it had no fins or scales. It was a bikini top! She and the guys exchanged looks. Weird.

Quinn twisted the stripped ends of the wires together. Then she touched a newly created circuit with the metal part of her knife. It sparked! Excellent!

Nicole, Michael, and Dana stared at the giant pile of wood on the sand.

"Pretty good, huh?" Nicole said.

Dana pushed her sunglasses onto the top of her head. "Really good," she agreed.

"Yeah!" Michael was pretty psyched. The pile looked great. "So" — he eyed the wood warily — "how do we light it?"

Dana shrugged. She'd never been much of a Girl Scout or a camper. "I dunno," she admitted.

"No idea," Nicole said with a forlorn shake of her head.

All three stared at the mass of driftwood.

Michael lifted a finger in the air. "All right, let's think. We're in the middle of nowhere, no matches, no lighter. How do we start a fire?"

More staring. And then, all together they yelled, "Quiiiinnnnnn!"

Quinn looked up from her work and saw the other kids waving her over. She got to her feet. "Yeah?" she asked, walking over as fast as she could. She was almost ready to try and make a call!

Michael got right to the point. "How do you start a fire?" he asked.

"Hmmmm," Quinn looked thoughtful behind her tortoiseshell frames. "Anybody got a mirror?" she inquired.

Nicole pondered this. She'd almost brought one, but... "Check Logan's backpack," she suggested.

Dana had no idea how a mirror was going to help, but she unzipped the main pocket and rummaged around in the pack. Resisting the urge to be really nosy, she just felt around for something hard and smooth. A second later, she pulled out a round hand mirror. "Leave it to Logan to bring a mirror to the beach," she said, rolling her eyes.

Quinn held out her hand and wiggled her fingers. "Gimme," she said.

Dana tossed the mirror, and Quinn caught it easily. Looking up, she examined the placement of the sun in the sky. She held up the mirror just so. She took off her glasses and held them about a foot and a half away from the mirror.

Michael, Dana, and Nicole looked on eagerly. Was this really going to work?

"Wait for it," Quinn said proudly. Nobody thought she was weird now.

They all stared at the pile of wood. A wisp of smoke rose up from the bottom. Then a red spot appeared and began to glow. Finally, the red spot burst into flames.

Quinn grinned as the others held up their hands to warm them. "There ya go," she said, slipping her glasses back onto her face. She handed Michael the mirror and turned back. Her other science project was waiting!

Michael watched Quinn go, then stared at the flickering flames in front of him. He was feeling nice and cozy already. "She's weird, but she comes in handy," he said.

The girls giggled and warmed their cold hands.

A little closer to the water, something tugged on the end of the fishing line — hard. Zoey, Chase, and Logan all reeled it in, and a few minutes later a three-foot fish was flopping all over the sand. Zoey blinked in surprise, practically jumping up and down. The fishers high-fived excitedly. Dinner had arrived!

Everyone sat together around a smoldering bonfire. They used sticks as skewers and were roasting the freshly caught fish to sizzling perfection.

"You know, usually I don't like fish, but this fish rocks," Nicole said, taking a bite of the roasted fish. It was definitely the best fish she'd ever tasted. "Doesn't this fish rock?"

Zoey nodded. She'd never caught a fish this big before, and it was awesome. "This fish rocks," she agreed.

"Hey!" a voice called from the ocean. Dustin. "Can I have some fish?" he asked, his stomach rumbling almost as loud as the waves.

"Sure!" Nicole said. It was a big fish — there was plenty for everyone!

Chase picked up a hunk of freshly cooked fish and heaved it like a football toward Dustin. Reaching high over his head, Dustin caught it and popped it into his mouth. "Thank you!" he called between chews.

Chase grinned and sat back down. There was some very delicious fish waiting.

"You know, this day started out pretty bad, but I really had fun." Zoey looked around at her friends. Who'd have thought that after one semester at PCA she'd have so many good ones?

"So, you girls aren't bummed that you missed the big PCA Mystic Beach party after-exam tradition?" Chase asked a little sheepishly. After all, it was the girls' first one.

Zoey shook her head and smiled. "No, we started our own tradition," she said. It seemed as though the girls had done a lot of that so far this year, and it was one of the things she loved about being in the first class of PCA girls. They were bucking tradition and making their own way!

"Yeah," Michael agreed as his piece of fish sizzled over the fire. "I say we do this every semester after exams."

Zoey raised her roasting stick. "A toast!" she said happily. "To our new after-exam tradition!"

"Cheers!" They all touched their roasting sticks together.

"Cheers!" Zoey echoed.

"Cheers!" Dustin shouted from the waves.

Everyone took a big bite of fish.

Chase was still chewing when Quinn rushed up to them carrying her newly created communications device. "I got it!" she exclaimed excitedly. "I think I've increased the cell phone's range by over four hundred percent!"

Chase eyed his cell phone, which had been ripped open and was now attached to Michael's computer by three dangling wires. "Aw, my cell phone!" he griped.

"My laptop!" Michael groaned.

"Oh, quit whining," Quinn ordered. What was their problem? She'd invented a device that would get them back to PCA, for goodness' sake! "Now, who should I call?" she inquired.

"Call a bathing suit store!" Dustin yelled over the surf.

Logan looked around warily. The sun was starting to set, and the last thing he wanted was to be out here all night. "Just call someone, because it's gonna be dark soon," he said.

"Hey, I know who we should call!" Chase said suddenly.

"Mister Bender!" Zoey said, catching Chase's drift.

"Yep!" Chase nodded.

Logan looked at Chase like he'd just said they should call a Martian. "He's a *teacher.*" He emphasized the last word like Chase had never heard of one before.

"He's a cool teacher," Chase said, pointing out the difference. He looked over at Quinn. "His number's programmed into my cell. Call him."

Quinn scrolled down the screen on Chase's barely intact phone until she found Mr. Bender's name. She hit SEND.

Rescue Party

A little less than an hour later, an old-fashioned blue pickup truck pulled in next to the beach. Zoey had never been so happy to see a teacher in her life — especially one as cool as Mr. Bender.

The kids cheered at the sight of their rescuer. Mr. Bender just smiled. "All right, let's see. Did someone need a lift?" he asked.

"Yeah!" everyone chorused as they leaned over the edge of the truck bed — everyone except Dustin, at least.

"Thank you so much for coming to get us," Zoey said gratefully.

"Sure," Mr. Bender replied. He reached into the back of the truck. "I brought those pants you asked for." He held up a large pair of khaki pants and looked around. "Where's your little brother?"

Zoey smirked. "He's still in the ocean."

Mr. Bender nodded. "Interesting," he murmured.

"Michael's watchin' him," Chase explained. "So just give 'em here and I'll help him get dressed!"

Mr. Bender handed over the pants and Chase ran toward the ocean.

"Hurry! It's getting cold!" Zoey prodded.

"All right, adolescents, climb in," Mr. Bender said. "We have a long ride back to PCA."

Zoey settled into a corner of the truck bed. "Quinn, I gotta say thanks," Zoey said gratefully.

"Yeah," Nicole agreed. "If it wasn't for you, we never would have had this" — she searched for the right word — "experience," she finished.

Dana nodded. "Yeah, thanks, Quinn."

Quinn held up the vial of her newly created chemical. "Oh, don't thank me," she said with a crooked smile. "You can thank my new synthetic coconut-smelling goo."

"Yeah," Zoey said with a grimace. "Put that away."

"Right," Quinn agreed, remembering all the trouble the little vial had caused.

Mr. Bender started up the engine.

"Wait!" a chorus of voices called from the beach. "Don't leave us!" It was Chase and Michael, who were pulling Dustin along, holding up the giant pair of khakis. They all piled into the back of the truck.

"Dustin!" Zoey cried as her little brother settled in next to Dana. "Your toes look like raisins!"

"You try bein' in the ocean for six hours!" Dustin replied a little hotly for a freezing kid.

Logan sifted through the stuff in his backpack. "Hey!" he griped as the truck pulled onto the road back to PCA. "Who got fingerprints on my mirror?"

Mr. Bender pulled into the PCA campus and parked the truck. Getting out of the driver's seat, he went around back to say good-bye to the kids.

"Okay, we're here," he said, closing the driver's door. Right away, he noticed that the kids were very, very quiet. "We're back at PCA."

Silence.

Confused, Mr. Bender pulled a flashlight out of his glove compartment and turned it on. He shined it around the bed of the truck. The kids were all fast asleep — and Logan was snoring!

"Hello?" Mr. Bender called out. "Let's go. Up and at 'em, guys!"

There was no response. Shining the flashlight over

the kids one last time, Mr. Bender noticed a small vial next to Quinn. He picked it up and an inviting smell drifted past his nose.

"Mmmm," he murmured. "Is that coconut?" He took a good sniff, then another. He yawned as he walked over to a large potted plant at the bottom of the stairs to the PCA campus. "Man," he mumbled as sleepiness washed over him. "Oh, this looks comfy." He gazed down at the cement walkway. "All right, kids. I'm over here if you . . ." He yawned again, unable to go on. The kids had the right idea. A little nighty-night was just what he needed.

Hang with Zoey Anytime!

NICKELODEON

Zoey 101™

Available for the first time on DVD Spring 2006.

© 2005 Apollo Media. All Rights Reserved. Nickelodeon, Zoey 101 and all related titles, logos and characters are trademarks of Viacom International Inc. TM, ® & Copyright © 2005 by Paramount Pictures. All Rights Reserved.